Last Tango in Long Beach

Gerald Locklin

Spout Hill Press

Published January 2013

ISBN: 978-0615736204

Spout Hill Press
Walnut, California
SpoutHillPress.com

To John and Ann Brantingham.
To all those, real or imagined, whose names, real or
fictional, I have dropped within these pages.
To Wanda (not her real name): the One Who Got
Away.
To Wendy (who isn't Wanda).
And, always, to all my children, and their children,
and their children's children...

Amen.

Acknowledgements

A portion of this novella was published in Germany, many years ago, in an anthology entitled, *Black Box*, by Maro Verlag. I thank them for that and for publishing the German editions of three volumes of my fiction and poetry.

Foreward

Gerald Locklin's trilogy of novellas *The Case of the Missing Blue Volkswagen, Come Back Bear,* and *Last Tango in Long Beach* are steeped in the mythology created by popular culture, first with the detective novel and movie, second with the western, and now with the sex drama – a sub-genre so important to 1970s cinema.

Each of these works though explores a facet of humanity that their respective genres can help to explore. In *The Case of the Missing Blue Volkswagen,* we are able to go into the complex psychology of the narrator's childhood. *Come Back Bear* looks at issues of personal courage and responsibility just as the classic western does, especially *Shane.* With *Come Back Bear,* Locklin allows himself to explore the idea of the relationship.

And Bear's relationships are real enough not to be easy. In this novel, we see the close up reality of long term love and how difficult it can be.

But the novella is a tool, and Locklin knows how to use it. He uses the form to raise so much of what he is doing to the level of myth. Changing popular culture into myth would not be possible perhaps with a novel. It would last too long become redundant and difficult to take. The novella is a perfect length for this statement. And he is able to raise the

1

personal relationship, what we often see as every day mundania, to a mythic level.

And by doing so he gets to an essential truth of humanity: All of our relationships rise to the level of mythology to ourselves.

Last Tango in Long Beach is a beautiful book that I know you will enjoy.

--John Brantingham,
author of *Let Us All Pray
Now to Our Own Strange
Gods*

The Hired Dick

She opened the door of my office and said, "I need a dick."

"You came to the right place," I said; "I'm the best dick that ever was, is, or ever will be."

"I *want* a dick," she said.

"I am the once and future dick."

"I want *your* dick," she said.

"Oh," I said.

She undid her bra and let it drop to the floor. She had breasts like exotic fruit. Unfortunately I do not know dick about exotic fruit. So I cannot tell you what kind of exotic fruit her breasts were like. I suppose I could get out a thesaurus or botany textbook or Handbook of Erotic Similies and list a whole shitload of exotic fruit names for you. Then you could make up your own mind as to what exotic fruit her breasts most resembled. But already we are in danger of forgetting her breasts altogether in favor of some exotic agronimical obsession. We are not in the business of agri-business here. We are in the business of dicks.

So let's move on from her breasts.

Let's move lower.

After dropping her bra she dropped her skirt and then she climbed out of her skinny panties. She did not remove her garter belt, black stockings, or high heels. She strode to the wall, spread-eagled herself against it, and demanded of my poster of Alan Ladd in *The Glass Key*, "Give me good dick!"

When it became apparent that Alan would not be responding to her call for emergency assistance, I went to her and satisfied her in both orifices.

Yeah, I'd seen Dr. Art Ulene on the Eyewitness News warning that *no sex* was really safe and that I was engaging in some of the most dangerous forms and circumstances, but would *you* like to have Dr. Art Ulene's sex life?

Anyway, the broad was pretty happy with my ministrations, and I'll have to admit I was not at my worst, for once. The broad had definitely made my day. Now I wouldn't have to shoot anyone.

She stepped back into her fancy duds and said, "Not bad. Thanks. I'd heard you weren't worth shit."

"Well," I said, "you know, you win some and you lose some. Every dog has his day. There is a time for sewing and a time for ripping."

"Listen," she said, "there is a time for choking on clichés and a time for knowing which side of the check your bread is buttered on."

"The Czech?" I said. "How is the Prague Spring?"

"Alive and living in Paris," she said. "which is where we will have our Penultimate Tango once you have found my daughter for me."

"Penultimate?"

"One should never miss a chance," she said, "to use the word *penultimate*. Because, after all, how many chances will you have in your lifetime to use it?"

"And when will my Last Tango be?"

"Ask Black Orpheus."

"Black Orpheus?"

"But first find my daughter for me."

"Can't I have a clue?"

"Just one: she's a bimbo with a brain."

"That's all?"

"And this," she said, and she pressed a plane ticket into my palm.

World's Ugliest Airport

The ticket was for a flight from the Orange County Airport, a.k.a. the John Wayne Airport. It is the world's ugliest airport and least convenient airport. Let's put it this way: the bronze statue of John Wayne is the *least* unattractive thing about the airport and environs.

Still, while waiting for my characteristically delayed flight and munching a $45.00 hot dog, I had time to contrast the message of Dr. Art Ulene with that of Dylan Thomas' "If I Were Tickled by the Rub of Love."

I hope you will do so also.

Coals to Newcastle

The plane set down at Oakland's pleasant albeit slightly boutique-y International Airport. I lugged my flimsy, cheap athletic bag up the ramp, my shoulder stiffening slightly. I was not getting any younger. I did not enjoy travel much anymore. Fortunately, I was seldom afforded the opportunity. Very few towns need one more dick.

A Non-Phenomenon

I was feeling a bit naked sans weapon of any sort. Naturally I'd been unable to transport so much as a lock-back knife on the plane. But I'd consumed my customary brace of Jack Daniels and was thus feeling not altogether unequal to the task of fighting crime on relatively unfamiliar turf.

I caught the Air-BART van to the Coliseum BART station, where I made the connection with the Richmond train to Berkeley. The elevators from the enormous terminal ascended to the youthful punk culture of Shattuck Avenue. These were not the glamorized editions of Hollywood clubs, though, or of the university community a few blocks up the hill. Not the streamline surf-punks of Huntington Beach or the working class politicized punks of London. These were just bored, slightly drugged, disaffected kids to whom looking unattractive came easily. Most were white, not all. They were not typical of Berkeley, just one part of it. They were no threat to anyone except themselves; they didn't even notice as I passed among them. They possessed neither the old values nor any new ones, neither ideals nor materialism. They were not hanging out looking for action; they were just hanging out looking for nothing.

They were hardly even a phenomenon.

A Drink For Old Times' Sake

For old times' sake I stopped for a drink in the bar of the Shattuck Hotel. The bar was, as usual, in a state of renovation. The lobby of the hotel was, as usual, in a state of renovation. The ballroom of the hotel, which had hosted some damn good big-band jazz in its time, was, as usual, in a state of renovation. I supposed other parts of the hotel were in their customary states of renovation also.

The pensioners who used to be housed there by the city were no longer in evidence in the lobby, but they may have just been watching game shows in their rooms. They had always left their room doors open, as they moved communally from one t.v. to another, perhaps in a vain search for undiscovered programming.

The hotel bar was not a gay bar, but I recognized a couple of the theatrical homosexuals who called it home. There were fewer of them, though. Fewer everywhere except in the obituaries. The virus had struck at the height of the era of free love in gay circles, and by the time it had been publicized it was too late for a great many. The heterosexuals had at least a warning period during which to consider the precautions, to moderate their lifestyles. Fundamentalists, eschewing charity, ascribed the epidemic to God's visitation on the Unnatural. The

9

gays must have wondered what kind of god would give them their special inclinations and then attach such lethal consequences. Double jeopardy. A compounded felony. Injury added to insult.

I recalled sleepless nights at the Shattuck, perhaps the world's most poorly soundproofed hotel, with the stridency and gunfire of drug deals emanating from street corners and the yellow light of the street lamps filtering between inoperable window slats. Something stupidly adolescent on HBO. A bottle of bad Solera and a flap of Maalox on the bedstand.

I remembered the night I called Linda in Seattle, and she was not home, and it was the beginning of the end of the affair, and nearly the beginning of the end for me.

I remembered how horny for her I had been, to the extent that I had tried to get drunk enough to suggest mutual masturbation over the phone.

I didn't remember if I had masturbated anyway. Probably, because I remembered kneeling on the tiles of the bathroom cubit in the morning, convulsed with the dry heaves.

I remembered having a drink or two with a tall redhead at that table right over there and thinking that her body must be spectacular, Rubenesque in bed … but I had a plane to catch and she, coming off a divorce and nervous breakdown, had had some cautions anyway.

I decided one drink for Old Times' Sake in the bar of the Shattuck Hotel was enough.

Something Else For Old Times' Sake

I crossed Shattuck to the Trumpetvine Court and a sampler of Vivoli's ice cream. I had some berry-and-chocolate concoction that I'd never heard of. I like ice cream, but I seldom allow myself any, unless I'm on the wagon, because I drink thousands of calories as it is.

But this was in honor of Gene Dinielli, who had taught me the ritual of Vivoli's, as he had taught me so much about what makes the world go 'round, and how to mitigate its spin with courtesies, amenities, and kindness.

Don't Leave Home Without It

I had packed my own half-gallon of Ernest and
Julio Gallo's Livingston Cellars Cream Sherry, so I
made no purchase at the Trumpetvine wine store. And
since I was getting a bit anxious about checking in, I
decided against drinks at the Bistro, a dive-bar in the
English sense, or the other truly American low-life
dive a block down form the monumental block-long
Shattuck Hotel.

Instead I dragged my bag and aching feet up
Durant Avenue to the classic hotel—a block above
Telegraph, a block from the campus—similarly named
for Henry Durant.

My room was waiting for me.

The Cause Of One Form Of Urban Crime

Hotel rooms promise so much and deliver so little.

Motel rooms promise a bit less and deliver a lot less.

This is why so many towels are stolen from both.

Also, the hotel and motel towels are invariably plusher than even the richest of us are used to at home.

A Modern Henry Clay

I took a quick shower, almost scalding myself, and stood naked and slightly dripping next to my bag as I pondered a change into fresh clothes.

I was traveling light and I'm not good at dealing with laundry.

I sniffed each of my used garments and decided on a clean shirt, clean jockey shorts, and the same pants and socks.

Man is a creature of compromises.

The Legacy Of The '60s

I decided to look for her first among the human detritus along Telegraph, although I knew it was unlikely I'd find someone of her youth among these dinosaurs of the 60s. I didn't reply to a single panhandler because you give to one, you got to give to all, and pretty soon you're taking personal responsibility for the starving trillions of Bangladesh.

For old times' sake I had a couple of Guinness Stouts, room temperature, in the once stately Hofbrauhaus now run by and Oriental family. Across the street at Larry Blake's, one could pay an admission to listen to bad jazz or worse poetry, but here, for no cover charge, I got to watch a druggie stumble in and collapse flat on his face. The police were called but they left the prostrate young man lying there while they negotiated a dispute at the curb involving a tow-truck which was attempting to remove an illegally parked car while its young female owner remained steadfastly behind the wheel. When it looked like the kicking of asses was about to begin, I finished my black beer and left. The sirens of paddy-wagons were audible throughout the quarter.

Still, it wasn't an easy job being a Berkeley cop. Berkeley was either the best place in the world or the worst place in the world to be a cop.

I wandered in and out of the bookstores of Berkeley, making sure that none of them had decided to carry any of the best young authors.

Of course they hadn't.

Authors from Southern California were especially notable for their absence unless they were Black, Chicano, Gay, Lesbian, Ex-Cons, Present-Cons, Future-Cons, or all of the above.

French post-post-deconstructionist critics were, however, very well represented.

I browsed through the literary theory sections because I find it so comforting to be reassured that I have an exceedingly problematical relationship to the hot lead that is frequently discharged in my direction as a reminder of the highest ontological questions.

I took an alternative route back to the hotel. It was designed to survey People's Park, the Symbolic Center of the Pro-Freudian, Pro-Peace, Anti-Authoritarian populist movements of Berkeley in the 1960s.

Now it was inhabited by fucked-up old men and fucked-up men old before their times. I'm not saying it was their fault they were fucked-up. I'm not saying it wasn't "society's" fault they were fucked-up. I'm not saying I'm not fucked-up myself. I'm not saying I won't one day be one of them myself.

I'm just trying to tell you what I saw. I know from my perusal of the post-post-deconstructionist works in the bookstores along Telegraph Avenue that no one else in the world might perceive People's Park exactly as I perceived it at that moment. I know that People's Park may not even exist.

I know that I may not even exist.

Horseshit.

I knew I was damned sure that the two guys a bit less (so far) fucked-up than the rest who emerged from the shadows and proceeded down the sidewalk towards me were perceived by me as having the distinct possibility of a mugging on their minds.

I became acutely aware of my lack of any form of hardware.

I crossed the street to where two couples were approaching.

I heard one of the perceived-to-be-would-be-muggers mutter, "Shit," and they disappeared into People's Park.

The Uglier Side Of A Hill

I can't tell you what it did to my self-image to
have crossed that street.
I, The Best Dick.
Sure, I didn't have a weapon, but …
Was I really feeling my age?
Had I lost my nerve?
Was I
    (gasp)
OVER THE HILL?

Communication Between Genders

I went back to my room and tried the t.v. No sports, unless you count Eskimo rugby, played with a recently deceased ball of fur.

I swallowed two quick slugs of Ernest and Julio Gallo's Livingston Cellars Cream Sherry, and I picked up the phone. I dialed Seattle. When I asked for Linda, the girl at the other end of the line said, "She doesn't live here anymore, but I recognize your voice, Dickenstein, and your lizard could shrivel before I'd give you her number."

"You're exciting when you're angry," I said.

"Putz."

"What are you wearing? Do you have big boobs or little titties? Feel free to talk dirty to me. What do you fantasize when you play with your clit?"

"You incredible primordial slug!"

"Tell me what it was like when you and Linda used to play with each other. No, don't bother to protest—I'm sure you did it all the time. Who went down on whom? I know she loved her pussy sucked. But she also like to take it in the ass. And what would you have to offer—a pianist's fingers when she was used to a pile driver. And what about unsafe sex and the threat of AIDS?"

"Do you have any idea how long you could spend in jail for the last thirty seconds of scum-palate assault?"

"Just think to yourself—he is entering me ... he is forcing his maleness up my docile, shameful nether entrance. I surrender my womanhood to him without reservation ..."

"HOW DO YOU KNOW THIS CALL IS NOT BEING TRACED??"

"Because that's not necessary. I'm calling from Room 518 at the Durant Hotel, Durant Avenue, Berkeley ..."

"Dick ... Linda's gone ... she's not coming back ... and she and I never had anything going on ... honest ... but you know that ..."

"Yes."

"So you won't call again?"

"No. Never again."

"Thank you. I never really badtalked you, Dick. It was just that I knew you were never going to leave your wife for Linda, and so she obviously had to circulate as freely as possible and find someone ..."

"Cunt. Jealous cunt. You'll never have with anyone male or female or hermaphrodite what Linda and I had."

"That's it, the last straw, I'm notifying the..."

SMASH!

21

A Bimbo With An Interesting Name

It was a minute of two after I'd hung up before I noticed my red message light was blinking. I lifted the receiver: "Yes?"

"There's a young lady waiting for you in the bar."

"She didn't leave a name?"

"Well ... in a way, but I'm sure she was putting us on. She said she was of the mixed blood of the three great Czech clans: the Wheat Chex, the Corn Chex, and the Rice Chex."

"Thank you—I'll be right down."

A Bimbo With A Brain

"Wanda, how did you know I was in Berkeley?"

"Oh, my mother called me. My mother doesn't leave much to chance."

"You mean your mother hired me to find you, knowing what had gone on between us, knowing I was in love with you, and not bothering to tell me it was you that I was looking for."

"My mother doesn't know as much as she thinks she does, or as she wishes she did."

"Your mother is a very attractive woman."

"How I hate that word *attractive*. Men are always telling me I'm *attractive*, and all they mean is that I'm not very beautiful but that I'm not so ugly that they wouldn't want to fuck me."

"You are, to me, *the entirely beautiful. Lay your sleeping head, my love, human on my faithless arm. Time and fevers burn away…*"

"Yes, I know, Auden. But I think ol' Wyston Hugh was addressing a man, wasn't he? Not that it wasn't his right to do so. Not that it would be frowned on in *my* neighborhood."

"He was addressing, on our behalf, whomever of whatever gender we long to address, I think. But why am I lecturing you—you're a poetess."

"I think the feminine diminutives are frowned on in these parts."

"Then NOW should place a dictionary with the imprimatur of that renowned linguist Gloria Steinem in every hotel room alongside the Gideon Bible."

"Bear, you know feminism has never been an issue between us. Aren't you even glad to see me?"

"*Glad to see you*? Wanda, when I overspeak myself, you tell me not to get too slimy, and then you present me with the most ridiculous question this side of a world that has not been proved to have any meaning beyond human caring. *Ah, love, let us be true to one another, for this world that seems to lie before us like a land of ...*"

"Levi's 501 prewashed jeans ..."

"Exactly. Wanda, I've told you that, excepting my children, you're the only person I've said 'I love you' to in ten years ... and it's only because my youngest children trust my explicit promise to them not to leave them no matter what involvement arises in my life that I can't follow that 'I love you' with some natural corollary like, 'And so I want to marry you,' or 'I want us to have kids together,' or 'Let's run away together to Paris,' or 'I want to make you the center of my life,' or 'Nothing matters to me except you' ... because a lot of other people *have* to matter to me."

"And so it's 'I love you so why don't we fuck.'"

"Give me a break, Wanda. It's been thirty years since I had to tell a girl I loved her to get into her pants. And anyway, we've already fucked, although I don't flatter myself that it rated among your top ten evenings spent in bed."

"How did it rate among yours?"

"How do you think it did? I lost you that evening."

"Oh shit, Bear, it wasn't you. It takes me six months to get to know someone well enough to want to do things with them, and then I'm immediately sorry that I did."

"I wanted you so badly … and yet I was so jealous … ah, fuck it … look, my heart leaps up to heights Wordsworth never imagined the minute I'm in your presence. You're like the first drink after ten years on the wagon. I feel your fingernails on my shoulder or hear your smartass voice on the phone or get one of your Dadaist home-made postcards in the mail and the universe takes on about eight new dimensions, like in string theory. Aside from you mother putting private eyes on your tail, are things okay for you up here?"

"Oh, yeah. I'm writing and I have a cheap pad with a roommate—female—that has a good sense of humor and I have a job that's stupid but easy and pays enough to get by, and it ain't the 60s and flowers in your hair, but there are a few things going on …"

25

"Wanda, I love you so goddamn much that I want…"

"That you want to fuck me in your hotel room."

"Listen, why did your mother hire me to find you, and what the fuck does she expect you to do now that I have?"

"You mean you haven't caught on yet?"

"No, I'm a-fucking-fraid I haven't."

"My mother wants you dead."

Hit The Deck

It was then that the lights went out and the machine gun fire commenced.

I dove beneath the table and felt around for Wanda, but she was nowhere to be felt. I swear if I had gotten my hands on her, I would have fucked her right there in the dark in the mayhem.

It would have been our *Last Tango in Berkeley*.

But her tits were nowhere to be copped, and my eyes were welling with tears as I listened to the shattering of the 12-to-20-year-old bottles of whisky on the highest tier of Henry Durant's fine old oaken bar.

It seemed like thirty years and three hundred jillion rounds of ammunition before police sirens could be discerned in the amplitude of their approach. The lights went on and I found myself the last person in the place. I scurried like a crab to the elevator to avoid the filing of a report with the police.

The Phenomenology Of Wanda

I suppose you'd like some idea of what Wanda looked like. I suppose you feel that narrators have some sort of unwritten (aren't they all) obligation to provide descriptions of their characters. I suppose you've always taken it for granted that narrators, not to mention dicks, possess superior powers of description.

Well, I possess no such powers whatsoever. I have virtually no visual memory or visual imagination. Also, I distrust adjectives. And I'm convinced that phenomena change their appearances before our very eyes.

I'm sure I could not give a satisfactory description of her (or of anyone) to the police.

Of course, I wouldn't, even if I could.

I'm sure I could identify her in a police lineup. Especially if I were allowed to cop a feel here or there as required.

And anyway, I've already told you all you needed to know: that she was a bimbo with a brain.

Except that that is not true. She did her darndest to play the bimbo—those high heels and tight pants and clown-colored socks and tee shirts and scarves. And the obligatory sunglasses and piled up hair. And lots of eye makeup and nail polish.

She did everything she knew how to look like a bimbo, and quite a bit to act the bimbo, too.

But she was NOT A BIMBO!

She was a brilliant and talented and beautiful and extremely well-read and extremely well-informed young lady and the bimbo business was one part defense mechanism and one part fun and one part mask in Yeats' understanding of the concept.

And I never saw her, clothed or naked, at any hour of the day or night, that she was not Auden's *entirely beautiful* to me.

And, of course, I was in love with her.

Still am.

And always will be.

And Then Of Course ...

… There was her tattoo.
But more of that later.
Maybe.
If it becomes necessary to the plot.

A Dick Travels On His Stomach

These days, almost literally.

At any rate, as eager as I was to make sure that Wanda was all right, I just couldn't pass up the Complimentary Continental Breakfast in Henry Durant's Pub.

The point is, not only was it complimentary, it was also free.

Croissants, bran muffins, jams and jellies from the farm of Walter Knott, choice of three juices, choice of fresh fruit. Good coffee.

I had to show my room key to prove that I was not a derelict off Telegraph.

I had a couple of croissants with butter and jelly partly in preparation for the augured Penultimate Tango in Paris, and partly just to jolt my pancreas out of its lethargy. We tough guys do, in fact, eat very little quiche, but only because there is usually something more interesting on the menu. In Paris, quiche is something everyone eats as a snack on the way home from work—something to tide a body over till dinner. The bakeries and the street vendors are ready with their slices for the rush hour. But we real men eat croissants, because excellent croissants and brioches are very excellent indeed, and French butter, and a big bowl of *café* with all the *lait* and tropical *sucre* one could desire. We tough guys have all read

Gertrude Stein's reminiscences of WWII, where she says the three things the French could not live without are butter, cream, and eggs.

Although I know a bran muffin and/or a piece of raw fruit would contribute to regularity of the bow-wows, I instead tell myself that I will take a portion of salad later in the day. I do not drink orange juice because citric acid gives me heartburn. I do not drink apple juice because, while delicious, it is also constipating. I do not drink tomato juice, in spite of my passion for it, because it gives me the runs.

Ordinarily I do not drink coffee, unless I need it to stay awake, because it burns a hole in my esophagus, most likely an incipient hiatal hernia. But I cannot pass up *good* coffee, because it is so seldom one encounters it. I pour myself half a cup and fill the rest up with cream.

There are complimentary newspapers (which are not only complimentary but free). I read the sports section, exulting where the Bay Area writers are saddened, and *vice versa*. Also, the Yankees have won and the Angels have lost. My day is made.

Do I seem to be neglecting my quest for Wanda? Remember, I am The Best Dick. I am *The Dick*.

And are you sick of me talking to you?

Are you sick of metafiction and post-metafiction and post-post-metafiction?

32

Are you sick of structuralism, post-structuralism, and post-post-structuralism?

Well, then, FUCK YOU, PAL. BECAUSE THIS IS THE ONLY KIND OF GODDAMN NOVEL I CAN WRITE! AND I CAN ASSURE YOU I AM JUST NOT RICH OR FAMOUS ENOUGH TO GIVE A FUCK WHETHER OR NOT YOU EVER READ ANOTHER WORD I WRITE.

So piss off, pal, with your oh-so-fashionable antipathy to "-isms."

The curse of literature is the reader (or writer or reviewer) who's taken one course in everything.

I'm not talking about the people who have taken no courses in anything or a lot of courses in a lot of things. Without these two classes of people there would be no literature at all.

But of the dilettantes, Al Pope once remarked that they should all go stick their heads in the Pierian Spring and drown.

Chinoiserie

Continental Breakfasts might as well be called Chinese Breakfasts because, as tasty as they are, they sure don't stick to the ribs.

I was, for instance, only a block down Durant from the Durant when my nostrils led me into the compact premises of that sausage emporium known as The Top Dog.

I can never pass up The Top Dog. If I had just emerged, stuffed like a Sonoma goat-cheese calzone from *Chez Panisse*, I would probably be unable to pass The Top Dog without darting in for a "Brat" and a "Cal."

There are rituals to be observed here. You never order a smoked Bratwurst or a Calabrese; you order a Brat and a Cal. Similarly, you call for a "Kiel," a "Top" (Frisco Style), a "New York," (although I've never personally overheard anyone order one), a "Knock" (-wurst), or "German," etc. From the clippings tacked to the walls, the ownership would appear to be of the Libertarian Party, and the cooks do not solicit the opinions of the clientele as to the quality of the cuisine, service, prices, or anything else. You pay when you place your order, and your sausages take their place on the assembly line of grilling sausages. Pots of sauerkraut, relish, and assorted mustards are free for the dipping. Non-sulfite potato salad, chips, and non-alcoholic beverages are available for purchase. Only the employees consume alcoholic beverages on the premises.

If you have been to Berkeley and you have not eaten at the Top Dog, you have not been to Berkeley.

The Haight Of Insolence

I hailed a taxi and commanded, "The Haight!"

The cabbie said, "The Haight'll cost you about forty bucks plus tip."

"Thank you," I said, and got back out of the cab.

Overdressed

I took BART to the Civic Center and walked a few blocks to the Haight. I was quickly assumed to be in quest of cocaine and was advised of the location of Crack Alley. Since I was a mere pedestrian and not commanding an armored battering ram, I did not attempt to search any of the Rock Houses.

Business did seem to be brisk, but I had an innate trust that Wanda was off drugs.

I asked around a little, but no one was volunteering any answers. That's when I knew that locating Wanda was not going to be as easy as I had assumed it would be.

Still, it was pleasant enough to have an excuse to wander around Haight-Ashbury and the Park. The gulls were still dive-bombing Kezar Stadium, but very few of the citizens were wearing flowers in their hair. None, in fact.

So I removed the gladioluses I had been wearing.

The City

It was supposed to be one of the world's most beautiful cities, but to me it had always been a sad sorry joke. The joke was on the people who *needed* so badly to think they were living in a very beautiful and special place. They thought that living there somehow compensated for the things that were lacking in themselves. They were foolish enough to think that choosing to live in "The City" conferred upon them some sort of superiority.

Talk about Vanity Fair. Talk about choosing the easy way out.

I had always considered the Golden Gate Bridge the world's ugliest and I had often tried to strike up conversations in the singles bars of The City with opening lines such as, "Why couldn't they have shown a little imagination, maybe filigreed it up a little like the Brooklyn Bridge, instead of just laying down one long boring arch of concrete?"

I never got laid much in San Francisco, a fact for which I am now significantly grateful.

At any rate, it used to be possible to make a case for the physical beauty of San Francisco, but that is not true any longer. The skyline is dominated, indeed obliterated, by bank buildings. Poverty and crime sprawl beneath them. The bay is discolored by landfill and chemicals. Activity in the arts grew inbred

38

and feeble. The groups who first enjoyed tolerance here have grown powerful and intolerant.

Of the era of peace, love, freedom, joy, poetry, and music, all that is missing is peace, love, freedom, joy, poetry, and music.

The intellectual climate is a vast circle-jerk over non-issues or the easiest of issues:

"Do we all agree that Apartheid is inhumane?"

"Ohhhhhhhhh … Yessssssssss …"

"What about gay rights?"

"Ohhhhhhhhh … Yessssssssss …"

"What about WOMEN'S RIGHTS?"

"OHHHHH, YES YES YES YES YES YES …!"

Unanimity. A city in love with itself in Collective Simultaneous Orgasm …

But, in reality, nothing happening. A city over the hill. Over its many hills.

With one thing remaining from the 1960s: The Weather.

Something Remains

I have lost a lot the last few years—I have lost a
lot of myself—but I have not lost everything.
Something told me to return to Southern California.
An inner voice I had always trusted.
A voice I decided to trust once again.
A trustfulness that almost did me under.

Homeward Bound

I checked out of the Durant and caught an early flight out of the Oakland Airport, a stroke of luck because you can go broke drinking in airport bars and you would never consider *eating* in an airport restaurant. I did have one drink while the plane was taxiing to the gate, and I overheard a family man tell the aging Southern waitress not to make his drink too strong.

"Honey," she answered him, "you don't never want to order a weak drink in a joint like this, because you can be damned sure you ain't going to get anything *but!*"

I had so far failed in my mission, but it was still great to arrive back with the sun still up and two little bottles of Wild Turkey in my belly. I had only my carry-on bag, and the long-term parking shuttle was waiting when I emerged from the terminal.

I stowed my bag on the passenger seat and hit the accelerator four, five, six times. Then I turned the key. It ignited instantly. I let the engine warm for a minute, shifted to reverse, and the car snapped dead.

The White Toyota Bites The Dust

This had happened before and the old engine had always responded after a patch of delicate footsying. But this time I wasn't confident: There had been something definitive about that snap. Sure enough, after a half hour of grinding the ignition with a foot now on, now off, now angrily pumping the accelerator, I gave up and went in search of a pay phone.

Your Friends In Need

The friendly auto club dispatcher gave me six
locations at the airport at which the tow truck would be
willing to meet me.

I was not familiar with any of them.

"Hang on a second," I said, and I went to check
with the Middle Eastern kid in the ticket booth. He'd
never heard of any of them either.

The dispatcher was growing impatient: "You
could call me back, sir, after you have oriented
yourself."

"That could be years," I said.

"What was that?" she asked.

"Nothing," I said. "What was the name of that
aircraft company?"

"The Fly by Day or Night Company?"

"That's the one. I'll find it. Dispatch your
mercenaries."

Sometimes Life Seems So Simple

I ran out to a parked taxi and asked, "Where's the Fly by Day or Night Aircraft Company?"

He looked at me as if I were daft: "Right behind you. See?"

An enormous banner covered the second story of the two-story building. It read: "If you plan to fly by either day or night, then fly the Fly by Day or Night Company."

I thanked the cabbie and went to stand in front of it.

A Semiological Mess

I waited twenty minutes without sighting any tow trucks. There was only one other person on the premises. He was working on a boat. Did I think it strange that someone was working on a boat in front of the Fly by Day or Night Aircraft Company? If you think that I would find such a thing strange, then you have never been a dick.

I did, however, find that I was in dire need of taking a piss. The airport and airline cocktails.

I went up to the man who was working on his boat and said, "Would you mind my using the men's room of your aircraft factory?"

"Aircraft factory?" he said. "Does this look like a fucking B-1 bomber that I'm working on?"

"What about the goddamn banner?"

"Oh," he said, "we let the aircraft factory fly their advertising from our premises. And we fly ours from theirs."

"What's the name of your boat company?"

"Sink or Swim, Incorporated."

"So when I find a building flying an enormous banner advertising Sink or Swim, Incorporated, I will know that I'm in front of the Fly by Day or Night Company?"

"That's right, mate. It's beyond those congested walkways and boarding zones in the farthest possible corner of the grounds."

Rabbit Rundown

I arrived out of breath and wheezing. The tow truck was just pulling in. The young man driving it bore physical resemblance to the criminals transported by England to her colonies over a period of centuries. His eyes twitched like the March Hare's. But the blood of no poet flowed in those taut veins. In spite of his obvious contempt for me for needing his assistance, I was glad he was what he was: a Machine Man. As Norman Mailer once dubbed Cassius Clay a genius of the body, so I predicted to myself that this inhumanist, this man for our times with the mental agility of a lug wrench, would have my car purring in no time flat.

He was worthless. After half an hour spent incapacitating nearly every still moving part of my vehicle, he got it going well enough for me to inch it to the toll gate. There it died again, blocking the exit, and the Middle Eastern cashier, perhaps a former repairer of tanks for one of Israel's enemies, proceeded to complete the task of incapacitation begun by the younger, stupider cousin of Rabbit Angstrom.

It took another forty-five minutes for Rabbit, myself, and his dispatcher to negotiate a deal by which I and my dead Toyota would be transported to Long Beach for a hundred bucks.

I tried to convince myself that Wanda's mother might pick up the towing tab, maybe buy me a new car.

A Sentimental Parting

Needless to say, I did not accomplish a great deal of searching for Wanda in the next few days.

It took a week and a half for the service station to which I had had the car towed to ascertain that fixing it (the timing chain, for starters, no pun intended) would be prohibitively expensive, but to get it operating at least where I could drive it home. But I dared not drive it anywhere else. My tax man said, "You can donate it to the Salvation Navy and write it off at Blue Book."

I unloaded it that day to good people who seemed to understand full well that what charity came their way had originated at home.

A young black guy drove me home. Naturally we discussed the only subject whites ever discuss with blacks: basketball. The separation between Lakers' fans and Celtics' fans is much greater than that between blacks and whites.

Ho Chi's Revenge

I decided to purchase for the first time in my life a brand new car. Only one even advertised within my price range: that spiffy new import from Hanoi, *The Tet Offensive*.

Wheel Deal

I had the cabbie drop me off a few blocks south of the Tet of Downey dealership. I didn't want the salesman to be able to tell how desperate I was for wheels. Besides, I needed to pick up some money at the bank.

The base model Offensive was advertised at $5195.00. Wandering around the lot, however, I didn't find a sticker under $7000.00, and that included most of the late model used cars. Eventually I was approached by a glad-handing young salesman who, when he heard how low my upper limit was, insisted we test drive a two-year-old Tercel that barely made it around the block. "Steve" kept insisting, "We must have gotten some bad gas."

"I don't want it. I know exactly what I want. I want the base model Tet Offensive for $5195.00."

"We don't have a single one on the lot. They don't make many more than the ones you see in the commercials."

"Can't you order me one?"

"Look, we'll fix everything on the Tercel before you take delivery. Five thousand even and out of here. It's still under warranty to Toyota, but you write up any guarantee you want and we'll sign it."

I started walking off the lot. "I guess I'll have to go to Tet of Hawaiian Gardens."

"Wait! Come on inside and I'll write up an order on a base model Offensive."

A Popular Color

"What color do you want?"

I asked myself what my little girl would answer if I asked her that same question and I said, "Red."

"Good thing."

"Why?"

"It's the only color they come in."

Closing

He was gone a long time to the manager's office where I knew he was smoking a cigarette, sipping a cup of coffee, calling his girlfriend, and generally killing time while he observed the protocol of letting the customer stew. Finally he returned and said, "I've got you one but you've got to take these four options for an additional $595.00."

"I don't need any steenkeeng options."

"Who cares? They won't sell the car unless you accept the options."

"That's bait-and-switch."

"So what?"

"You're advertising a car you won't sell."

"You gotta read the small print in the advertising."

"What're the options?"

"Wheel trim, door trim, trim trim, and a dental plan."

"A dental plan?"

"You get 50 bucks if your teeth get knocked out while driving past a V.A. Hospital. The Tet Offensive is still experiencing some resistance among less enlightened elements in the community."

"Together those options are worth about ten bucks."

"It's where we make our profit. C'mon, I need to sell two more cars today to buy my girl an engagement ring."

I checked out the bottom line: $6525.00.

"That's *it*? No hidden charges? Tax, license, dealer prep, your rinky-dink options, the works?"

"Not a penny more. No one in America will buy a new car cheaper than you this year."

"Okay, write it up."

"How do you intend to pay?"

"Cash."

"You mean *check*?"

"No, I mean cash." I took out my bulging wallet and peeled off the amount in six T-bills, five C-notes, two twenties, and a five.

"You always carry that much cash?"

"Nah, I knocked over a small bank on the way this morning. Afterwards there were a million cop cars and helicopters searching for the getaway car, setting up roadblocks, and everything, but since I was just a harmless pedestrian, no one even noticed me."

"Yeah, sure, ha ha ha ha ha. It's a good story, though. Incidentally, how come you didn't try to get a trade-in allowance on your present car?"

"I don't own a present car. But what would you have given me on a '77 Toyota station wagon that doesn't exactly run?"

55

"We would've given you a couple hundred off and then we would've found a way to add it back on."

"That's what I figured."

"Hey," Steve said, "since you obviously consider us a bunch of crooks, why didn't you go to a different dealership?"

"Can you give me the name of a dealership where they *aren't* crooks?"

Steve smiled.

"How soon will the car be delivered?"

"Actually, you can take delivery in ten minutes."

I smiled.

On the way to the car we passed a t.v. in the finance office. Police were winding down their search for the getaway car and were investigating the possibility that the robber had fled on foot.

Steve smiled.

I winked.

Sweets To The Sweet

No sooner had I arrived home than UPS was delivering a box of chocolate chip cookies with a request that I fill out and return a customer satisfaction questionnaire. I opened the cookies and ripped up the questionnaire.

A few days later another box of cookies and questionnaire arrived.

I opened the cookies and tossed the questionnaire.

Did they really think I was stupid enough to either (1) compromise any complaints I might have about the car or the sales methods by singing its praises so soon or (2) leave myself open to a slander suit by making charges that I might not be able to prove?

They were damn good chocolate chip cookies. I wondered who the baker was for Tet Offensive of Downey.

The Return Of Laura

I was about to recommence my search for Wanda, when there was a faint knock on my office door. Through the marbled glass I recognized the statuesque silhouette. Laura had come back to me.

"Come in," I said.

"Are you glad to see me?"

"Of course," I said.

"I mean … I really didn't behave quite …"

"Ancient history …"

"I was so young …"

"Water over the dam."

"I loved you *too much*."

"Shhhh."

"I was so jealous of your wife. I was so inexperienced myself … I had to learn more about life … and love … myself … so that I could understand *you*."

"Wonderful."

"I knew you were furious. I know I hurt you terribly."

"Not a word of it."

"But now I am prepared to come to you, as your peer, in the powerful and profound complexity of the love between a strong, mature man and an equally strong and mature woman."

I began to pull the king size Murphy bed down from the wall.

"Already?"

"It will be the altar for the silent trothing of our newer, truer love."

I slid her jeans down and off and got on my hands and knees in front of her. As she stood there, Junoesque, I licked the inside of her legs from ankles to panties. Then I lay her back on the bed, her feet still on the floor, pulled her panties aside, and sucked on her clitoris. At first I held her to my face, her surprisingly narrow buttocks cupped in my hands, but soon I ran my fingers up under her T-shirt to pinch her nipples through her bra.

When cunnilingus had taken her as far as I wanted it to, I lifted her legs onto the bed, undressed myself, and standing next to her rubbed the head of my penis lightly back and forth across her lips. Because she wanted to take it into her mouth, I would not let her. Instead, I got between her legs and, once again just pulling her legs aside, I slipped it to her. I thrust in stops and starts, accelerating the tempo and then bringing her to an abrupt halt, letting her sit as at a stop light, wondering how much longer before the light would change and it would start again. Sometimes I held myself above her like a cobra; other times I let myself down to hold her head to the bed by the hair and insert my tongue in her ear. I thought of tying her to the bed by her hair. Maybe later.

I slipped her panties down and off one leg, but left them dangling from the other ankle. As I stroked I would run her panties up and down the length of that leg. Periodically I would, still in her, massage her clit with her panties. Or I would shove them up her ass, then yank them out like a rip-cord.

For a long time I lay at different angles to her, as in the Kama Sutra, while touching her in different places.

Sometimes I allowed her to do things of her own volition, like raising herself up to bite my nipples, but I always pushed her back down before there was any question of who was in charge.

She did not try to sit atop me, because she did not like the way her heavy breasts hung down. She did not like me leaving her shirt and bra on her either, because she thought this meant that I did not like her big tits, that I preferred my wife's tight little ones. Actually that had nothing to do with it. It simply accentuated the nakedness of her bottom while her top remained clothed, and it added another sweet stage to the ungarbing.

When I had allowed her to remove her blouse, I pulled the straps of her bra down about her arms so that she remained bound by it even as her nipples slipped free. After I removed her bra and held her entire body against mine, I began to practice a technique imparted years ago by my black spiritual advisor, Brother Lloyd. I thrust my cock not into her but up and down against her clitoris, so she felt it grow larger and hotter. I lubricated my hand from her cunt and ran a finger deep into her ass.

Eventually I pulled her to the edge of the bed, stood there holding her legs straight up into the air, and began fucking her in the ass. I knew this was what she really loved, this was what she had been waiting for—it was most likely why she had come back to me—because everyone was too scared to practice this unsafest of sex. But I figured that, in spite of the efforts of the gay community to counteract the conception of AIDS as a homosexual disease, that heterosexuals would still be relatively safe for at least a couple more years.

So I drove deep into her, burying her head and torso beneath me, and as I could feel her muscles tightening and hear her voice loosening towards climax, I pulled out of her and let my sperm cascade down as from a fireman's hose upon her thwarted and still sizzling body.

"What are you doing? Are you crazy? Do something for *me!*"

"Sure," I said. I pulled on my own pants, gathered hers up in my arms, and walked to the door. I opened it, threw her T-shirt out into the corridor.

"Bear!" she said, "I love you. I've come back to you. Don't do this to me."

"Hurry up," I said, and tossed her jeans far down the hall.

"You said you forgave me!"

"I lied." The bra followed the jeans.

"Bear, we are great together! This is the greatest sex either one of us has ever had. Are you willing to throw all this away for the rest of your life? We've only just begun experimenting ..."

"You threw it away," I said, and I flung her panties and shoes out of the room.

She made the rush of a madwoman at me then, but I sidestepped like a Tai Chi master and, with the aid of a foot to her lower back, sent her sprawling onto the outer floor. I locked all the locks behind her, went to the phone and pretended to ring up the police, "There's a naked woman ranting outside my office. No, honest! Yes, I assume that she's on drugs. Thank you, better hurry, be on your guard, I think she's dangerous."

The noises she made departing the building were of no animal I had ever previously encountered.

I went to the window and opened it. She was half-dressed and searching for the key of a sporty little Honda. "Incidentally," I called down to her, "all those years that I insisted that I wasn't sleeping with my wife ... *I was lying*!"

The Hunt Re-commences

I was sitting at my desk sipping a whiskey and trying to decide where to re-commence my search for Wanda when the mailman delivered a letter with no return address. I ripped it open and recognized the handwriting. It read, "Come and get me, Dick."

I wondered who had forced her to write it. The complimentary close read, "Always your betty-def and fresh and waiting."

That was Wanda all right—reggae had been replaced by rap.

But I still didn't know where to look for her.

The letter was signed, "Wanda Jean Murrieta."

Oh-oh! I was about to have to relive what was probably the most stress-laden journey of my life.

It Begins

I spent the first night at a county campground at Diaz Lake, two miles south of Lone Pine. As usual, it had been an awful drive across the Mojave Desert, hot and boring, the heat slapping against the left eye, left ear, and left side of the face, the boredom against the right. But it had been no worse than many such trips and a little less than some. That was the problem with taking trips out of L.A.—no matter where you wanted to go, you had to cross an immense desert to get there. It was a fact of life that had kept James M. Cain and Raymond Chandler and John Fante and Joan Didion and John Gregory Dunne in business, but it was a simple imposition to the rest of the population.

You say you love deserts?

Yeah, well, so do I, the Sonora, for example, around Tucson.

But I don't love the Mojave.

I parked my car in a campsite as far away as possible from what seemed like potential partiers, deposited my six dollars in the fee slot, and walked down to the edge of the lake—really just a pond—where we had let the kids wade in up to their ankles.

I had asked them not to go in water above their knees, and so they of course had to test what constituted the tops of their knees.

I had asked them not to go too near the cattail swamp, and so they all but disappeared among the bulrushes.

The shore baked with insect food for the varieties of land-and-sea birds. Two striking orange-headed blackbirds nested in the water growth.

"When I was growing up and fishing all the time," I said to my wife, "do you know where the fish always hung out?"

She didn't really care—she would rather have answered, "Who gives a fuck?"—but since it was only the first day's late afternoon, she had asked, "Where?"

"Wherever you couldn't get at them without snagging your hook and having to cut it loose."

She said nothing. Looked away towards the kids. Snapped her camera.

She began that evening, putting up the tent in a strong wind, bitching about having to do everything herself.

"You don't do everything yourself," I said, and held one of my children to me with each arm. You certainly don't pay your share, I thought, although you like to pretend you do. You put up the goddamn tent and you move things around in the car.

I could see it starting, and I didn't remember ever having seen it start so soon, and I wanted to give us all every chance. So I held the kids and kept my mouth shut.

Later, when everyone else was in the tent, I sat up trying to read Wallace Stegner's *Angle of Repose* by the halogen lamp, but it attracted every insect in the Owens Valley. I set the lamp aside and read as well as possible by flashlight and reading glasses. Heard noises behind me. No, too deliberate to be the wind. Tried to catch it with the flashlight glare. Finally did: a mother skunk, her paws frozen in the air, her child already inching away from the trash cans to follow here back over the fallen log. I read some more, drank some more cream sherry, climbed into the back of the station wagon to sleep.

Perfunctory Chapter

The next morning I took the kids back to the lake while Brenda decamped and packed. I knew she wasn't feeling well. Female problems. Hormone pills. And the customary sinus pills and Excedrin.

She'd given up smoking years before and drank half a beer before bed.

The overloaded Toyota made it through the Alabama Hills and up the sheer expanse to the trout pond, waterfall, and the trail heads of the Mt. Whitney Portal.

Two weeks later a busload of Marines descending the Whitney Portal road would take an accelerating corner too fast and go rolling off the edge.

Later we would find a campsite near a lake at Mammoth and drive down to the Devil's Postpile.

Bad ribs at a redneck joint in town.

Mosquitos as big as B-1 bombers. No reading at the picnic table tonight.

Too complicated to read in the back of the wagon.

Just consume as soon as possible enough cream sherry to forget the bear warnings—*lock all food in your car*—and that you will be sleeping with the food in the unlocked car—that *you* are bear food.

And to sleep.

Tufa The Seesaw

Do you know what tufa is?

It's this stuff found in formations at Mono Lake. The cool spring water meets the hot surface water and there's all this salt involved and before you know it you have tufa.

Today's first science lecture.

Mono Lake has special significance to a dick because of the diversions of water to L.A., and all the fortunes made à la *Chinatown*, one of the great dick films of all time.

The shore of Mono Lake is infested with sand fleas, although nowhere near as badly as the Great Salt Lake. And since it is the last refuge of a lot of bird species, you tend to be happy about the abundant if not entirely ubiquitous bug food.

You see, it is a myth that all dicks are anti-ecological. Most of us, in fact, are totemic, and thus we long for the perpetuation of the Bear, the Wolf, the Eagle, the Coyote, the Tapeworm.

The *Tapeworm*? Ha, ha, I just slipped that one in to make sure you were still paying attention.

Even The Ghosts Have Moved On

From just north of Mono Lake we headed east into the foothills to Bodie. Ten years ago, as I have stated elsewhere and elsewhere, I wouldn't drive my wife's then new Toyota into Bodie because the road was so rough for so long. But now all except the last three miles of the road have been paved. The woman at the Bodie museum tells me the last three miles were left unpaved so that the tourists could get some small sampling of the experience of traveling in the Gold Rush era, before either automobiles or paved roads came to California.

I tell her I think I and my wife's now maturing Toyota could have gotten the value of the experience from maybe a final thirty unpaved yards.

Joaquin Got Around

Bodie is a pretty nice town, mostly because nobody lives there except a couple of rangers, and it wouldn't frankly surprise me if the rangers had a residence in about thirteen other ghost towns as well.

Bodie has a lot of authentically western stories to tell, such as the death of the variously spelled William Bodey for whom it was named. It also, needless to say, insists upon having been a frequent hangout of the bandit Joaquin Murrieta.

Offhand, I can't think of a town in the Mother Lode that doesn't claim to have been frequented by the bandit Joaquin Murrieta.

My wife was once taking a course in California History for Teachers and as the instructor was lecturing on Joaquin Murrieta, my wife glanced over and noticed the veteran teacher next to her writing something in her notebook about "the banding *Walking* Murrieta."

Well, Joaquin didn't walk, he rode a horse, the best that he could steal, and he sure as fuck did get around, if one is to believe the chambers of commerce of the Mother Lode.

And as for the woman who wrote down *Walking* Murrieta, I guess that's not so bad: she might have gone off to teach her fourth grade class a unit on the half-breed Chinese bandit, Wah King Murrieta, presumably the brother of Chun King.

I Can't Do Everything At Once

I know you're complaining, "What about your kids? How come you never tell us anything about your kids? If you're going to introduce your kids into the story, you know, you've forfeited your right to protect their privacy."

To which I say, Cow Plop! I don't have to tell you a single fucking thing more than I want to! And it's not as if I haven't told you plenty about some of the other characters, myself included.

Yes, it will be necessary to reintroduce my beloved children into this tale in just a few minutes. But you may rest assured that, as proud as I am of them, I will give you just as little of them as is absolutely necessary for the telling of what I have set out to tell. That concluded, I shall remove them from literature and deport them back where they belong, among kids their own age, none of whom, I trust, is a reader of this saga.

The Sonora Pass

The woman in the museum in Bodie had told
me, "Yeah, you can probably make the Sonora Pass in
your Toyota, and it's beautiful this time of year, what
with the Aspens and everything, but you really ought
to go back and cross by the Tioga Pass. It's just as
high, but it's a lot more gradual."

We had been to Yosemite numerous times,
though, and to Mariposa, Hornitos, and Coulterville at
the southern end of Route 49, so within an hour we
were nearly sliding back out of first gear while
simultaneously nearly boiling and going over the cliff
of the Sonora Pass, resplendent with Aspens and with
peachfuzz Marines from the Mountain Warfare
Training Center.

The kids, playing a game of make-believe in the
back seat, sensed no danger.

When we accomplished the summit, my wife
and I, in a rare display of camaraderie, speculated over
what mountainous terrain the President was planning
to send America's youth to die in next. And for what:
coffee beans, cocaine, caviar? There aren't any oil
wells at 10,000 feet, are there?

And there were Washington Irving
thunderstorms.

While beneath us, the Stanislaus River and its
tributaries made believers of us that California—the

physical California, the irrigated California, the thirsty urban California—could actually have occurred.

East Sonora Idyll

Fortunately we did not have great difficulty in finding an affordable (thirty-seven dollars as opposed to six bucks a night at a campsite) motel. The kids and I repaired immediately to the surprisingly lengthy pool while my wife availed herself of a long hot shower. There was sibling competition for the father's attention in the pool, but we all survived it. We wore ourselves out.

Later we found a family restaurant which was cheap and had the kind of food that kids will eat, and where I did not even feel the need of the alcohol they did not serve.

Real food, real toilets, real beds, real television, real showers, real air conditioning, real breakfast— what a deserved respite in civilization, the kids and I enthusiastically, and my wife begrudgingly, agreed.

But even she was in a good mood.

It was one of those together evenings that restores your belief in families as a positive phenomenon.

It was the calm before the storm.

The Case Of The Missing Gas Cap

Friday began auspiciously. We got a rested and refreshed and yet reasonably (for us) early start to Columbia City State Historical Park, a ghost town operated, unlike Bodie, for profit, and yet not without historical authenticity. The kids took a stagecoach ride and sampled sarsaparilla in the saloon. It was so hot that I allowed myself a couple of Henry Weinhard Irish Ales with lunch. Later the kids panned for gold, and for a couple of bucks more the management will make sure there's a fleck of two of the precious metal in your dirt. As usual it took Brenda an infinity to negotiate the gift shops, but I was happy enough sitting on a bench and reading about the bandit Joaquin Murrieta's frequent visits to Columbia. I was happy because it was turning out a good day for the kids.

Brenda was considerate enough to make short shrift of the old church and courtyard—we wanted to stand a chance of getting a campsite at Calaveras Big Trees State Park. Compared to, for instance, those operated by the National Forest Service, a California State campground is a veritable Ritz, replete with hot showers, flush toilets, drinking water, spacious sites, and other such amenities. Consequently they're a little more expensive and a lot more popular.

We took Parrot's Ferry Road, the scenic route, the back road, with its bridge across the Stanislaus

River. Outside of Murphys I almost got a ticket for driving on the shoulder to let a line of rush hour traffic pass—one that included a county sheriff. I pulled into a small shopping center to see what he was going to do, and when he decided to shine me on, I figured we might as well fill the tank and stock up on soft drinks. Until now, I had been going inside to pay while Brenda pumped the gas, but this time she had some other things she wanted to look for.

When she came back I said, "You know the gas cap is gone?"

"It's been gone a long time."

"Did I lose it that day I borrowed your car?" I added, because I knew I was capable of leaving gas caps on the tops of Toyotas as I drove off.

"No, you didn't lose it."

She was getting angry, I could tell. She doesn't like to admit that she ever does anything stupid like the rest of us mortals, and so she was getting pissed at me because I was indirectly dwelling on her having done something stupid. So I just said, "We'd better find a parts store in the morning. Gas caps are cheap." And I pulled back onto the highway.

Within twenty minutes we were being told by the two attractive park rangers that we should have availed ourselves of their reservation system but that yes, if we would pull our car over to that lot on the hill,

I could return and register for one of their three remaining campsites.

I parked quickly and hustled back by myself, but then, knowing Brenda, I wasn't comfortable selecting the site without her—whichever one I chose would prove to have major drawbacks in her estimation—at it had also occurred to me that we should perhaps take a place for two nights rather than face the paucity of Saturday night accomodations. I turned to wave for Brenda to join me, but she was already pointing frantically at the rear end of the car. It looked as if she were pointing at the tire, but the tire didn't appear flat. I hate public displays and shouting across great distances, so I waved more adamantly for her to join me. Agitated, she rushed to do so: "The car is leaking!"

Now I did see a spreading flood across the black asphalt.

"Shit," I said, "it's probably just an overflow from the gas tank. I shouldn't have filled it so full."

"It isn't stopping!"

A man walked up and joined the line: "Do you folks know you have a gas leak—that's mighty dangerous."

"The gas cap is missing," I said.

"Oh," he said, implying, *Then why don't you get a new one? And stop polluting our fresh air and endangering your family.*

"I've got to get the kids out of there!" my wife cried and went running frantically back.

It was my turn in line, so I picked the site that seemed closest to the showers and paid for one night only. Then I returned to the now-empty car. At first I was afraid the leak was actually in the tank, in which case the trip was as good as over, but I traced it to the missing gas cap. It had just about stopped dripping now.

I got in the car, let it roll back to level ground, and started it as a demonstration it would not go up in flames. I knew, of course, that all this time that I did not know the gas cap was missing, an overflow onto hot metal could have sent us all up in flames. This was also a possible explanation for the poor mileage and low power. And hadn't it ever occurred to her that you're not supposed to get dirt or moisture in your tank? I guessed that she had figured the little metal door that locked shut was protection enough.

That could have been the end of it, except that Brenda had decided that the only way to avoid blame in our eyes—no one else was interested in blaming her—was somehow to make me the villain. So when I asked her if it looked like I was going the right way on the park map, she snarled, "How am I supposed to know?" And she re-opened her door and slammed it.

"What's all that for?"

"What?"

"All the slamming and everything."

"What was all the snapping for all day?"

"What snapping?"

"All day long you were snapping at us. I couldn't do anything right all day."

"Oh, for Christ's sake."

When we parked at the campsite, she stayed in the car a long time seething. The kids wanted to play in the meadow, so I walked down to it with them. When they had to go to the restrooms, I went with them. My heart wasn't in the trip much anymore, though. I stayed at the picnic table while they played there, and then I went to the head myself to give Brenda a chance to emerge from the car without losing face. She took advantage of the opportunity to unpack the necessities and to take the kids with her to a big fallen log across the meadow. I returned to the picnic table and poured myself a drink.

She would have liked to have cut me out of the cold-cut supper, with no restaurant or store to run to, but since we were sharing all costs, I just helped myself to my share.

She would have liked to have refused to rearrange things from the trunk of the station wagon to the back, but she probably knew I was already planning to just dump all her stuff out on the ground if she tried that.

As she put the tent up and transformed the station wagon, the kids sat on my lap at the picnic table. Later, at a private moment, I asked Missy, "Was I snapping at your mother today?"

And she said, "I didn't hear it, but Mommie always says you're not as nice to her when we're not around as when we are."

Incidentally, the sleeping in the car bit was not purely a matter of exclusion of me or of her not wanting to deal with a second tent. The last time I camped on the ground at Big Sur, the dampness got into the arthritis in my lower back to where I had to inch out of the tent on my stomach like a snake and then wriggle across the ground to a tree by which I could pull myself to my feet with my arms. Brenda brought me the miracle drug Motrin and a Coke to swallow it with and I was at least able to hobble along with them to the Monterey Bay Aquarium, my beloved daughter leading me as if she were my staff. Since then, I've pitched my sleeping bag in the back of the wagon.

The Worst Day Ever

Saturday morning Brenda was still slamming car doors and throwing things around and bitching sotto voce while taking down the tent and packing the car. Jack ran about with his toys, oblivious in the space-forest of his imagination. Missy sat in my arms at the table and waited for Brenda's temper to run its course, although we had both seen that take weeks on occasion. My wife did not offer me any of the bear claws that she had purchased for breakfast at the market in Murphys. Brenda, incidentally, is not a bacon-and-eggs person. She is a chicken-and-fish vegetarian. I would bet anything she read in some women's mag that it was a way of retarding cellulite. And it has largely worked. She's a little thing, less than a hundred pounds, but she always has been anyway, and her mother, who is not a vegetarian but whose appetites are almost as atrophied as Brenda's, is a life-long stringbean also.

Anyway, you might think Brenda's vegetarianism would translate into a healthy diet for the kids, but joined with her hatred of cooking it really comes down to, except for the occasional meal, a diet of fast food and sweets. You would cry if I described their typical schoolyear breakfast. Honest to God, I'm lazy too, but they'd be better off with *me* feeding them.

So why don't I?

That, as you will see, is the classic Brenda double-bind: She gets stuck doing everything, but of course, nobody's assistance could ever satisfy her standards anyway.

Somehow, though, this time she calmed down once we were back on the highway. Probably her Excedrin and antihistamines and hormone pill and sugar-fix began to click in. And I pulled over at an auto parts store in Arnold and replaced the gas cap for $3.50.

We'd been to Mercer Caverns before, but that was ten years ago with two of my children by a previous marriage. At any rate, I remembered it as a place that would make a big impression on a kid. And I thought I remembered talk of the bandit Joaquin Murrieta having hidden out there. So we drove the one mile out of Murphys to it.

Afterwards, the car seemed to be exhibiting an oil leak, but that proved to be a false alarm.

Have you heard tell of E. Clampum Vitus? They're apparently a bunch of historically-minded and civic-minded wiseacres who came up with the Twainesque idea of preserving the West in a manner that mixes Dada with Rotarianism. I kind of liked the idea. One of their headquarters is the Murphys museum, whose outside is plastered with plaques to themselves.

Besides the building itself, the best things about lunch at the Murphys hotel were the ice water and the glassware it was served in.

On to Angel's Camp, of Jumping Frog fame. Except for the annual contest, not much of interest.

Same for most of this middle portion of Rt. 49.

Mokolumne Hill—just call it Mok Hill—had possibilities that are currently unrealized. Jackson still had The National Hotel, but Brenda and I had already been there, and to the honky-tonk bars as well, and the kids opted for soda fountain root beer floats. Then off to find a place for the night.

The kids were begging for a motel. I couldn't find a decent campground listed that wasn't fifty miles out of our way. Brenda admitted she was feeling so awful that she'd willingly go halves on a motel. We headed for Placerville, through some lovely orchard hills, in the best spirit of cooperation.

Unfortunately, it was hard even to find a motel row in that freeway-canyoned junction. When we did, the two remaining rooms were overpriced and too small at that. We decided, the parents still bound in unanimity, to try our luck farther up Highway 49.

There were no inns between Placerville and Coloma, site of what is now known as Marshall Gold Discovery State Historical Park, also known as Sutter's Mill, the place the Gold Rush started and one we could not drive past. Even at this hour of the early evening it was overrun—with river rafters. Apparently the South Fork of the American River was the equivalent for Northern California of what Lake Havasu and "The River"—the Colorado River—were to their counterpart revelers to the south. We drove to the edge of town and back without encountering a regular motel, just what seemed a lodge with no vacancies and a couple of private campgrounds back in along the river that most likely did not have vacancies either. We came to the dirt road up to one and I said, "Do we try it?"

"What do you think?"

"I think if it's not full it's probably a rip-off, but it's getting late and who knows where we'll find a place on a Saturday night. And we want the kids to see Sutter's Mill, don't we?"

"Yes."

"Do I try it—I'm blocking traffic?"

"I suppose so."

I parked in front of the office and went in alone. It looked like no one for miles was over twenty-five. The girl behind the desk said, yes, there were three sites left at $12.00 a night, but we should go check them out first. There was one nearer the restrooms, but there was a bachelor party in progress next to it. Yes, there was a pool, but it was down by the river and cost extra. Yes, there were showers, but only a couple.

Yes, there was a mini-market—literally minimal—and a 4-stool beer bar adjoining.

This was not the Taj Majal of campgrounds, but it was a place to park for the night and surprisingly cheap. I went outside to tell Brenda and the kids. Brenda did not look happy that they had a vacancy.

We found a site overlooking a ravine and a good walk from any convenience but not adjoining any orgies.

"Do I take it?"

"Do we have a choice?"

"I don't know."

"I wish there were an alternative."

"Can you think of any?"

She didn't answer.

"Do I take it?"

"I don't know. I suppose so."

"Are you sure?"

"I guess there isn't any choice."

"Then you stay here and I'll walk back to the office."

"We can drive."

"No, you and the kids need to get out of the car."

Naturally, I got lost once on the way down the hill (or hills), but I finally staked our claim to the inelegant campsite. Then I went next door for two quick draughts in the otherwise empty mini-bar while selecting one six-pack of beer and one of root beer. It was obvious we were going to have to find some place in the "town" to eat.

I trudge back up the dusty hill under the 90-degree sun with a six-pack dangling from each hand. When the kids see me coming they are excited, more by the root beer than by me. Brenda takes one look and says, "Oh, how nice, something for everyone except me."

"I picked what I thought everybody liked. I could only carry so much. I can go back for something else if you'd like."

She looks away towards the ravine where a mother quail is circling her young.

I sit down at the picnic table and open a beer for myself and root beer for Missy, Jack, and Brenda. Brenda doesn't even look at hers.

I begin to realize what we are in for.

Trumps

After a few seething minutes during which Missy grows quiet, her brother chatters on, and I try to swat honey bees away from the root beer, Brenda grabs her root beer long enough to swallow some pills, snarls, "I have a terrible headache," and leaps up to start spreading out the tent. Jack and Missy get up to help her, but she snaps at her daughter, "Will you please try to stay out of my way?" Then she says, "That's right, Jack, that's a big help holding that rod for me."

Missy comes to stand next to me and I hold her loosely inside one arm. Brenda trips over a fold in the tent and demands, "Do I have to do everything myself?" I get up and go to pick up one end of the canvas, but she yanks it away, "You're only making it worse!"

I drop the tent, and Missy, who has been on her way to pitch in, edges backwards.

"That's right—leave it all to me, as usual."

Now I'm beginning to see that there is literal method in her literal madness—as awful as she feels, she has nonetheless been fomenting a strategy into which I have allowed myself to be drawn. She is an almost unbeatable player of Chinese Checkers because she thinks twenty moves ahead and specializes in hooking her opponent on the horns of dilemmas—no-win situations. I step back and try to say as softly and dispassionately as possible, "Look, I know you haven't been feeling well and I sympathize with that, I honestly do. But you knew what chores were going to fall to you before we ever started on the trip, because they're just the same ones that always have. And you don't really want us to help you anyway. And I don't really want to get in a fight with you, but you started this business the very first night of the trip."

"Oh, so I'm a bitch all the time ... I've been a bitch the whole trip ..."

"Nobody's called you a bitch or any other name."

"Well, if I'm so horrible a person to live with, maybe we ought to just go home tomorrow."

"If you think we should go home tomorrow, I have no objection."

This stuns her just a flicker. Then, "Maybe this is the time for us to just split up right now!"

There it lies: The trump card has been played.

"No you don't," I say. "You don't pull that like you tried to pull it when we moved into the house last summer. You can leave me any time you want, but you're not leaving with the kids and you're not leaving with the car and stranding us out in the middle of nowhere."

The kids have run to the back seat of the car, so I go to them and do my best to explain things. Missy says, "I'm not leaving," and Jack says, "Me neither."

"Okay," I say, "I don't want anybody leaving anybody. I want us to all be together so stick to your guns, and I think it can still work out all right."

Brenda finishes with the tent. By now the kids and I have returned to the bench of the picnic table where I am facing away from the table with one child on each knee. Brenda storms to the car and says, "The children and I need showers."

"You're not going off with the kids in that car."

"You mean you don't even trust me to take them to the showers?"

"Didn't you just get done threatening to split?"

Missy says, "I don't want to take a shower."

Jack says, "Me neither."

Brenda stands by the car, foiled. I know how she must feel. It must be the most devastating moment of her life. I feel sorry for her, very sorry, but there's no way I could ever make her believe that. And it's too soon to let down one's guard.

She backs out recklessly and disappears over the hill in a cloud of dust. The children are terrified: "Do you think she's leaving?"

"She'll be back; she's just going to the showers." Then, having won this battle at least for my children, I begin to weep.

"Daddy, Daddy," my daughter says, "please, don't, or I'll start crying too."

My son is puzzled: "I didn't know that parents cried."

"They do," my daughter says, "but please stop—I'm afraid she'll come back and see you crying."

"I know," I say, "I know, but you two are everything to me and I've been so afraid she'd manage to take you away from me. And you handled everything perfectly—what courage that took because I know you love your mother very much and you don't want to lose her either. And you won't. But if you hadn't stuck by me—if she had thought for a second that she could take off with you—well, you know, she would have loved to leave me sitting here."

"I know. But what if she leaves us *all* sitting here. I don't even know where we are."

"I do. And it won't happen. But if it did, I have credit cards and checks and versateller and a couple hundred bucks. We'd spend as much as we had to to get out of this hole and we'd be home before she was."

"There she comes."

The Toyota skids into the dust. "Were the showers full?" I ask.

"Yes," she hisses, and although I'm no longer crying, she takes a look at my eyes and says, "You can

91

stop crying—I won't steal your precious babies from you."

And as she storms into the tent and fastens the flaps closed behind her, I don't bother to say, "I know you won't."

My Daughter And I

For a long time the three of us just sit there at the picnic table holding each other. Then in all the resiliency of childhood, the kids decide they want to play hide-and-seek. I supervise that they don't crash over the cliff or through the tent. Then, as Jack draws pictures, my little girl and I have a whispered conversation downwind from the tent: "I'm going to let her rest a while longer and then I'll invite her to go into town and get something to eat with us. If she refuses, we'll go without her."

"She gets like this and then it takes her forever to get over it. Why can't she just forget things quick like the rest of us?"

"It's the way she's always been. I've been with her for eighteen years."

"I've seen her bad but I've never seen her this bad before. She may *never* get over it this time."

"Oh, I think she'll get over it. Maybe not tonight, but maybe tomorrow. I hope so. God, Missy, I feel as awful as I've ever felt in my life. I have this terrible hole in the pit of my stomach. I never would have dreamed that children of mine would have to go through something like this. This trip is supposed to be for *you*—you're supposed to be having a great time, not enduring an ordeal …"

"Daddy, don't start crying again …"

"No, I won't this time. I won't say any more because no more is necessary and I don't want your mother to think we've all ganged up against her. Let's go back to the picnic table now and have another beer and another root beer before we ask your mother out to dinner ... but I want you to know that I realize what courage it took for you to stick up for me, and what would have happened if you didn't, and I promise you I'll never forget it."

A Familial Repast

She agrees to accompany us to town, but only in the worst of spirits. I find a place with a restaurant, bar, and a soda fountain that serves both sandwiches and wine. Brenda repairs immediately to the Ladies' Room. Missy returns, only to blurt, "She won't talk to me. She won't even look at me."

I say, "She'll be at her worst tonight."

The food orders get sent to the wrong kitchen and take forever to arrive, but at least I'm able to consume three wines in the meantime. I provide the kids with pens to draw on the placemats.

Although they do not finish their meals, I let them have dessert. God knows when their mother will be in the mood to feed them again. I keep them reassured with touches.

On the way into the campground, I get us lost. Brenda offers no assistance. I cannot believe how a mother can jeopardize her children for the sake of scoring points against her husband. I ask advice, get righted, and purchase a 1.75 liter bottle of rosé as insurance at the company store on the way to the campsite.

She does not help get her children ready for bed because she is trying to show them what life will be like with only a father. But they are capable of getting themselves ready anyway. I call to her in the tent,

"What are the sleeping arrangements?" and her voice cracks, "What do you mean?" For the first time I have the fear that instead of taking the children away from me, she may in fact be losing them. "Go sleep with your mother in the tent," I tell them. "I love you terribly and I'm sorry for tonight and I hope tomorrow will be a better day for all of us."

Rock Me, Emmanuel

I rearrange the station wagon for my sleeping bag with virtually no difficulty. I think I have made much easier work of it than she ever has.

Then I sit up sipping the abominable Almaden rosé in lieu of my beloved Ernest and Julio Gallo Livingston Cellars Cream Sherry. There is a large group partying at a double campsite catty-corner fifty yards up the hill. Eventually, though, I perceive that their not-all-that-loud music is Christian Rock: *Rock Me, Emmanuel.* Frankly, I am very grateful to have Christians, as opposed to, say, the Manson Family, camping in my neighborhood. Also, they turn out the lights precisely at midnight. And when I catch one couple sitting up late, and from this distance it seems as if they're making love in the Lotus position, the girl begins chanting, "Double-sixes, now, double-sixes, now, now, now, now, NOW …"

I realize they have been playing a hot game of dominoes.

Sunday

Brenda awakens me, slamming doors and suitcases.

I see her head over the hill to the restrooms.

I have had vastly inadequate sleep. I am hungover, depressed, exhausted, and distraught.

The kids are still asleep in the tent.

I have some serious decisions to make, one in particular.

Although it is daylight and the Christians are arising, I stroll nonchalantly to the ravine and take a nice long piss down it.

Then I return to the picnic table, pop a root beer, and wash down two Excedrin.

Then I return to the tailgate of the station wagon, check to see that the kids are still asleep and the Brenda is not returning from the lavatories, and, on one knee, chug-a-lug the rest of the rosé, about a quart of it.

I am not a person who greets each morning with a quart of wine. I know that should this scene be documented it could cost me my kids. I also know, however, that I have ironically taken the wisest, sanest, safest step possible under present conditions.

I toss the bottle down the ravine and go to rouse the kids.

Unfuckingbelievable

The kids tell me that their mother would not hug or kiss or hold them or even say goodnight at bedtime.

Now she still won't.

I get them some packaged things to eat and she packs the car.

We drive into Sutter's Mill. We tour briefly the Visitor Center and the park. I urge the kids to take up with her, but she refuses to let them join her. She walks off crazily in illogical directions to avoid them.

I know what this is doing to them, but I also know what an indelible education into herself she is providing them with.

Smart Kids

Since Brenda is refusing to talk, I am calling the shots by default. I decide to stop for lunch at a famous café in Auburn.

Just coincidentally the place serves wine. I order a gentleman's half-carafe of rosé and a grilled cheese sandwich. The kids order fruit salads, which I authorize. Brenda orders large and eats none of it, but I'm planning to charge her for it anyway. Let her pay for her petty gestures.

On the way out I dart into the liquor store next door in search of my beloved Cream Sherry. Consequently, Brenda and the kids get to the car ahead of me, and when I get there, Missy and Jack are crying. "Stop crying now," their mother is saying, obviously unwilling that I know what has transpired.

I don't think you want a report on the rest of our day in Grass Valley, Nevada City, and the Empire Mine—although I would recommend you not miss the Nevada City Museum, once the fire station, with its joss house exhibit in the rear of the first floor and its ghosts upstairs.

That evening, alone in the motel pool on the north outskirts of Sacramento, my little girl tells me, "When we got back in the car after lunch, she said, 'As soon as we get home I'm leaving, and you can both stay with your father.' And so Jack and I both cried and said, 'We don't want you to leave.' And she said, 'All right, stop crying, I won't leave then.'"

"You did the right thing. You did the perfect thing. That was exactly what she needed."

"She didn't want you to know."

"I won't let on. You did brilliantly."

"I really didn't want her to leave."

"I know you didn't. She's your mother. I want you to have your mother. But instinctively you kids did exactly the right thing to keep the family together."

"Will we get to see the State Capitol tomorrow?"

"Yes, and Sutter's Fort and the Indian Museum. You are an amazing kid, Missy, truly an amazing kid."

It's All Downhill From Here, Almost

Shortly after we returned to Long Beach, Brenda took off with the kids for our cabin at Big Bear. I knew I'd miss them, but I didn't worry about them. Brenda would be at her best, trying to bind them to her, hoping to rebuild her devastated bridges. That was fine with me. I hoped they had a wonderful time.

Certain things had been indelibly communicated.

Now, back at Diaz Lake, it was time for me to sally forth once again, in search of Wanda, as I had been commissioned, and in search of my own Terpsichorean Destiny.

But Where The Fuck Are We?

Where the fuck were we?
How the fuck did we get to where we are?
What tense are we in?
What is all this Last Tango horseshit?
How the fuck do I have any idea where in the world to look for Wanda?

I Had A Hunch

A hunch that I would find her in Emoryville.
Emoryville?
Emoryville is a largely abandoned warehouse
district between Oakland and Berkeley beneath the
Bay Bridge. America is, characteristically, replacing
an estuary.
I'm afraid if Jesus Fucking Christ came hopping
back on a sweet fucking stick and I asked him, "Are
you sure the rich won't inherit the earth?" he would
feign shock:
"Did I say that?"

It's Reminiscent Of An Old Ku Klux Klan Joke

You know, the one where Abraham Lincoln wakes up hungover after a three-day-binge, gets a quick briefing from his staff, and gasps, hair on end, "I freed the who?"

Or Did I Already Use This In Another Book?

And speaking of where the fuck we are, there's always the acorn about the Indian tribe, the Fukawees, and the Army tracker who went all over the West asking, "Where the Fukawee?"

All I Ask Is A Modicum Of Respect

Anyway, Emoryville is nothing but a marina, abandoned warehouses, a high-rise of condos, scattered yet-to-be occupied urban enclave one-way glass fully automated office buildings, a towering Holiday Inn, and other motels and restaurants at the level of originality of Trader Vic's and Denny's.

Denny's is less offensive because it's less expensive so I ate there.

Then I checked in at the Day's Inn, which, as a very funny guy named Ken Seib once said, may not have the world's smallest swimming pool, but probably has the only one with faucets.

The bar was the size of a breakfast nook and just as exciting. There were three dentists on a couch sipping margaritas in front of the silent small-screen t.v. after a hard day at a holistic root canal convention and even they looked bored.

The black bartender was as quiet as everything in the "bar" and was attired in a tuxedo that would have been the rage at my mother's senior prom. The cheapest drinks were five dollars and the bar was closed on weekends. Too noisy a place, no doubt, for either Sabbath. The dentists were trying to remember who had picked up last night's tab at Carlos O'Brien's.

The motel had room service but no restaurant. The smart money was on a shuttle service from that smart brasserie down the street operated by Monsieur de Denny.

I ordered a gin and tonic with lime and I'll have to admit it was perfectly prepared with the best of ingredients—as it should have been—commencing with Bombay gin. I complimented Uncle Tom and inquired, "Has Wanda been in?"

He bent close to my ear and whispered, "Sir, *no* unescorted ladies have been in."

Maybe it was the obsequious/superior way he said it, or maybe it was just that he had served the dentists little bowls of those tasty cheddar flavored goldfish while neglecting me, or maybe it was the way he had peered out the corner of his eyes at the rolled cuffs of my Levis and the missing buttons on my Taiwanese tennis shirts, but, for whatever reason, I sank my fingers into his wooly hair, tugged his face towards my lap, and demanded, "Have you sucked any unescorted dick lately?"

"N-n-no, sir."

"Then tell me where the fuck I can find Wanda."

"Try the new Italian café, sir—the little place up Powell Street."

Immediate Disclaimer

Now please let's not mistake the previous chapter as a slur upon blacks. One black does not the whole race make. I would rather you dwell on Martin Luther King, Jr. although I doubt Martin would have been caught dead is any place as dull as Emoryville. Martin was a great man, but he also liked a little action.

I wonder if it's where they invented the Emory board. Maybe Joe Niekro grew up there.

Anyway, please remember: all Italians are not Al Capone, nor are all Poles Popes, nor are all Irish drunken, vainglorious louts, although neither I nor my old schoolteacher at Sonnet Tech, William Butler Yeats, ever met a single one who wasn't.

Also, There Are No Drunken Indians
In Gallup, New Mexico

And politicians of all nations really do have balls, although not quite enough to go around.

The Arturo Toscanini of Junkyard Dogs

On Powell Street, beneath the underpass, I was accosted by assassins of many nations: It was kind of like a United Nations of Ninja. There must have been seven hundred of the murderous brigands and no two of the same race, creed, color, religion, national origin, or sex.

I decided first I'd try to settle the misunderstanding amicably, with a little humor: "Hey you guys," I said, "this anti-discriminatory make-up of your barbarous ranks ... it's really very white of you!"

That didn't provoke a chuckle.

So I tried, "Aren't you guys afraid of muggers?"

Believe it or not, that one got them thinking. They began exchanging whispers until finally one took on the role of spokesman: "We have decided—why would muggers come here when there's no one to mug?"

I didn't really have an answer for that one so I tried the old Mark Twain ploy: I brandished my knife and taunted, "Come and get me ... but whoever gets to me first is going back to his mother on his shield."

This one really got to them, temporarily at least. They went into caucus for a good twenty minutes. Most of them tearfully extracted photos of their moms from their wallets. A few were cursing that they'd left their shields at home. Finally, though, one young lion stumbled onto a brainstorm. He circulated his idea amongst his fellows and they all turned to face me, all seven hundred of them, with drawn guns: "We don' got no shields!"

It was at that moment I heard from just up the alley the barking and howling of five junkyard dogs and one human being. I knew it could only be my beloved friend Gene Dinielli.

He left the beasts to keep up the barking and howling without a conductor and came trudging slowly towards us wearing a fully-stocked grenade belt that wound round his waist and over his shoulder.

"I'd been saving these for our retirement trip to Northern Ireland," he said.

"Oh well," I said, "There's that one guy there right in the middle of the pack sporting his Ian Paisley T-shirt."

"Paisley," Gene said. "Italians never wear paisley. Why wear your sperm on your sleeve?"

And he extracted a grenade from his belt.

Afterwards he said, "There's this little Italian café back up Powell I want to introduce you to. *Prosciutto e melone*, washed down by Guinness on tap."

"I think that's the little Italian place on Powell Street to which I was on my way. Do you think you could get us past the local quintuplet of junkyard dogs?"

"We are members of the same glee club."

La Dolce Vita Nuova

At Carrera's Café, Dinielli forced upon me multiple orders of *prosciutto e melone e Smyrna fichi*, not to mention introducing me to polenta with pesto. In turn, I forced upon us numerous Guinness Stouts and Sierra Nevada Ales from the tap. Eventually I got around to asking if anyone matching Wanda's description had been in.

"Oh sure—she left just before you guys came in. She said if a big dick came in I should tell him to look for her at Wong's Bavarian Village. I guess I should have known you were the big dick that she was referring to."

"Wong's Bavarian Village?"

"That's right—they have the best Mexican food in Emoryville."

"Look," I said, "you don't let Italians in this place, do you?"

"Italians? Italians are all we let in. In fact, I'm Italian—*all of us* are Italian!"

"Gene," I said, "I hope you know the Italian for 'Shit, guys, I was just funnin' you.'"

What's In A Name

Naturally, Wanda had left Wong's Bavarian Village just before we arrived. She'd left a message to meet her at a bar a little farther up Powell called the Brick Slit House.

"Are you sure it's not the Brick *Shit* House?"

"No, they didn't want to name it anything crude."

The AIDS Age

On the way to the Brick Slit House, we passed a
cluster of prostitutes and their pimps giggling at the
corner of San Pablo. It seemed like a slow night. I'd
seen a recent t.v. special about heterosexual black men
who had contracted AIDS from the whores patrolling
the San Pablo beat, so I wasn't surprised that business
was slow. And I'll have to admit that if it weren't for
the AIDS threat, I would have pulled out twenty bucks
to back up one against a wall right there.

Last Ticket To Paris

The lady tender of the bar at the Brick Slit House said that Wanda had not been in but that a woman claiming to be Wanda's mother had been and that she had left me a plane ticket for a pre-ordained Tango in Paris. She handed me the envelope.

"Where do I go in Paris?"

"She said you'll be met at the airport by Philippe Noiret, Gerard Depardieu, and Jean Rochefort."

"Oh, good. Then I won't sweat it."

Telling the barmaid, "My friend's from out of town—his money's no good here—and one for yourself, please," Dinielli bought a round.

I looked around the bar, which seemed peopled with bikers, addicts, dealers, thieves, murderers, psychotics, and final-stage syphilitics, to the extent those forms are not overlapping. "Nice neighborhood bar you have here," I said to the barmaid.

"Yeah," she said, "no darkies."

I looked at Dinielli and our eyes said, "So much for the vaunted liberalism of the Bay Area." Dinielli said, "What about *Ark*ies?"

"Oh, sure, everyone here is an Arkie."

Dinielli raised his voice: "Has anyone in this joint ever heard of Jephtha Evans?"

There was no response.

"Is anyone here from Booneville?"

No response.

There were no more Arkies than Darkies in there.

We drank till closing.

Last Tango In Paris

To my inordinate surprise, I *was* met at Orly by Philippe Noiret, Gerard Depardieu, and Jean Rochefort.

"Jesus, guys," I said, "you guys are my favorite tough guys since Bogey. I mean, most of the Americans take themselves too seriously, and although I love the acting of Michael Caine and Bob Hoskins, I don't think I'd really want to *be* Michael Caine or Bob Hoskins. But you, Philippe, you prove it's possible to be middle-aged and out of shape and mildly corrupted and yet tough and, overall, a force for good; and you, Gerard, no one can kick down a door like you can— why you could kick a door down with your chin; and Jean, you are so sensitive, you are so weak, you are so stupid ..."

"That's enough for now, Dick."

"Then let's speed to the Left Bank ... or the Right Bank ... or any bank where I can exchange some currency ... and then we can begin kicking ass and taking names all over the city ... and I can find Wanda's mother and Wanda and call a few numbers that were left with me by expatriating literary types, and I can at last consummate my own Last Tango in Paris, and as aperitif, my Penultimate Tango in Paris, and, before that, my Ante-penultimate Tango in Paris, and ..."

"Gerry," they said.

"Gerry?" I echoed.

"Yes, Gerry. Not Bear, not Dick, just Gerry."

"Okay."

"There isn't any Paris."

"What?"

"Temporarily, at least. It's been taken out of circulation. Given a rest. Closed for renovation. Put on hold. Due to re-open in the year two-thousand-something."

"I don't believe it."

"It's true. For you, at least."

"Why?"

"You've had your Paris. You've been in love in Paris. You've written about it. Your Paris is gone. It's in what you've written and it's in the music of Gato Barbieri and it's in your love for our movies, it's in your memories, but there isn't any Paris *here* for you right now. Maybe someday, maybe once again, but not tonight. Not this month. Not this year. Maybe not this decade. You'd be fakin it—like Antonioni making *Zabriskie Point*."

"Then no Last Tango for me and Wanda in Paris?"

"Not this year."

"How about just a mini-Tango with Wanda's mother?"

"C'mon, Gerry. You met Wanda's mother once at a poetry reading. You found her mildly attractive for her age, but you knew it would be a traumatic betrayal of Wanda's trust to have anything to do with her, even to share her 'mature' view of Wanda's wanderings."

"Then Wanda doesn't *need* saving?"

"We all need saving. But no one can save us."

"Then Wanda doesn't even need me?"

"Of course she needs you."

"What can I do?"

"Go home. Be there when she calls you, to the extent you can do so without neglecting your own children. Make sure she understands that there are limits, that you'll never be her puppy dog. Get her used to the idea that there will be others. Mainly, try not to be an asshole."

"There will be others?"

"Of course."

"There are Tangoes yet to be Tangoed?"

"Naturally."

"What about my wife?"

"She's an asshole."

"Jesus, that's supposed to be *my* line. And her life is not an easy one, and I've hurt her a lot in the past, and ..."

"Yeah, but let's face it, she's dangerous—shit, we're not telling you anything you don't already know. Co-exist, but cover your flanks."

"Okay, but *merde*, I really feel bad I didn't get a chance to paint the town Toulouse-Lautrec with you guys."

"You will."

"But time passes."

"No it doesn't. This is still the start of a beautiful friendship."

"Tell me one more thing—am I, 'Gerry,' the Gerald Locklin who is the author of this fiction?"

"Yes and no."

In Long Beach We Tango
Like Every Tango Is Our Last

I arrived by Concorde at the Long Beach Airport. It had been a comfortable flight and I had been well attended. I had, in fact, been the only passenger.

The in-flight movie had been *Last Tango in Paris.* At my request it was shown three times.

I had long wanted to add a *Last Tango in Paris* number to my closing routines at poetry readings. People were getting tired of my Tap Dancing Poem and my rendition of Johnnie Ray's *Cry.*

But could I hum the music and dance the narrative at the same time?

Could I moon the Tango contest judge without getting either arrested or fired?

Could I count on my audience to summon up Maria Schneider in her full-thighed baby-flesh sensuality? How many would even have seen the film? Did I need a partner?

Wanda?

Wanda would have been perfect.

Wanda of the absolutely insignificant tattoo.

Wanda who, like Schneider, had, would have, had always had a slight tummy?

A tummy?

Had I ever knocked Wanda up?

What about all the months during which I hadn't seen her?

Would I ever know?

Was this why she wrote me once, "I read what you write about your children and I weep"?

I drove my red Hyundai home from the airport. My wife and kids were long asleep. There were two notes awaiting me.

The First Note Said,

"Missy says the lunch area at her new school is unsupervised. The older kids throw apples and other fruit around and make bombs out of drink boxes. Apparently one boy tried, maybe just kiddingly, to steal her lunch."

Reflexively, I reach for my gun.

Then I realize this is one of those innumerable modern problems that cannot be solved that easily.

This is one that will require phone calls to bureaucrats, one that I will, of course, come out of looking like a fool.

Well, not for the first time.

But how much easier it would be to just plug the unruly little bastards.

And if one had to deal with big assholes and too many of them—well, my eyes grew misty with thoughts of Gordoni the Crazy and Sergeant Roger Hotspur and Cowboy Bob and Big Ed and Ramon the Magnificent and Schweppervescence and the Two Tonys (Tony-Nice and Tony-Suave) and John Halloran and Bob Austin and Jim Jansen and so many other truly tough but equally good-hearted guys that I had run with in the old days who would ride into the teeth of death, a Wild Bunch to the finish, a Seventeen Samurai, a Magnificent Seventy, a Dirty Dozen-Dozen.

But what were we supposed to do—ride into town and stomp the shit out of the goddamn school board? Talk about a shit storm!

I was so upset by the idea of my daughter's being in even the slightest jeopardy that I knew not even booze would help my sleep.

I had two choices: Excedrin P.M. or a Joan Didion novel.

The Second Note

But just then I noticed The Second Note:

"Surprise. Number One Son called. You're going to be a grandfather in April."

I would not be a Dead Grandfather, not having pursued Maria/Wanda in my sybaritic folly up the spiral staircase to her flat, there to plant my spearmint underneath her banister before collapsing into anonymity.

One Two Three Four

One Two And Three Four

One Two Three Four

One Two And Three Four

In Long Beach we Tango as if every Tango is our last.

We howl with junkyard dogs.

Wanda, Wanda, Wanda.

It was time to go beyond Brando. I had been a terrible father to my oldest son, and then no father at all.

Once upon a time I had been The Best Dick.

Now it was incumbent upon me to become the best grandfather that my already reviving spirits would allow me to become.

About the Author

Gerald Locklin has published over one hundred volumes of poetry, fiction, and literary essays including *Charles Bukowski: A Sure Bet*, (Water Row Press) and *Go West, Young Toad*, (Water Row Press). Charles Bukowski called him "One of the great undiscovered talents of our time." *The Oxford Companion to Twentieth Century Literature in the English Language* calls him "a central figure in the vitality of Los Angeles writing." His works have been widely translated and he has given countless readings here and in England. He is a Professor Emeritus at California State University, Long Beach.